PUMPKIN SPICE AND ALL THINGS NICE

Cauldron Coffee Shop
Book 1

LAURA GREENWOOD

other updates, you can join my mailing list via my website or The Paranormal Council Reader Group on Facebook.

Blurb

When coffee shop owner, Willow, receives a mysterious teapot from her best friend, her charmed life is turned upside down.

Between the cursed warlock who thinks he's still in Ancient times, the cat who insists on coming through her window and making herself at home, and a new employee, Willow has her hands full.

Can she unravel the mess she's found herself in? And can she do it without losing her heart?

-

Pumpkin Spice and All Things Nice is

book one of the Cauldron Coffee Shop
Series, a witchy modern fantasy series
with a romantic sub-plot, a mysterious
teapot, and a cat who might be up to
no good.

Chapter 1

I sing to myself as I switch on the coffee maker and get ready for the day. There's plenty to do around here before the rush of customers who want to grab their morning perk up, and that keeps me on my toes for at least the first hour of the day. At least my new barista is starting this week. I was reluctant to bring anyone else into my business at first, but even with a good dose of magic, I can't keep up with the demand all the time.

The familiar gurgle of the water boiler soothes me in a weird way most people don't get. For me, it just reminds me that I'm safe in my own space.

The bell rings, and I glance in the direction of the door to see the local postman smiling and waving with a package in his hands.

Hmm, how odd. I'm not expecting anything. Maybe Sabine has sent me something from all the way around the world where she's studying some ancient ruins, a thousand-year-old dead witch, or something equally as weird and kind of interesting. I don't really understand half the things she says when she talks about her job. I just know there are a lot of graves and long-lost treasures involved.

Not my thing at all. But she's my best friend and it keeps her busy, even if her room in the flat remains empty as a result.

I pull my wand out of my pocket and fire off a quick spell at the door, unlatching the lock and making it swing open for the man.

"I'm never going to get used to you

doing that," the postie says with a wide grin.

"Sorry. Want a latte to take with you?" I need to remember that he's one of the humans that freaks out around spells. Not that I truly understand why, supernaturals have been out in the open for nearly two hundred years, which is much longer than he's been alive. A witch running a coffee shop is perfectly normal.

"You know I can't, but thanks for the offer." He sets down the package on the counter. "You need to sign."

I'm disappointed, but I know he's right. He's not allowed to accept it in case it's some kind of bribe. "All right."

He passes me the machine and I do a vague imitation of my signature. I don't understand why those things are used at all, my name never looks right on them, how can they possibly prove it's me who has signed it?

"I wonder what it is?" I muse, inspecting the package but not seeing anything useful on it other than a lot of stamps. Sabine may be the culprit after all.

He shrugs. "I'm just the messenger."

"Better get out of here so I don't shoot you if it's bad then," I quip.

He chuckles nervously and runs off pretty quickly. Huh, maybe someone has shot him for delivering bad post before. I bet it was a tax bill. No wonder they email them now.

I shake my head and turn my attention back to the package in front of me. I pick it up, and something rattles inside.

Hmm. That doesn't answer anything about it.

The coffee machine beeps, pulling my attention away. I can't let a package ruin the routine I've made for myself. I stick a mug under the spurt and press the next button. The first coffee of the day starts pouring out, filling the air with a familiar sharp and sweet scent. I take a deep breath, enjoying the familiar smell. The allure of good quality coffee never gets old.

I pick up the mug and grab the package, taking them both over to the small table next to the counter. I'll be able to look at it properly here while keeping an eye on the rest of the shop in case anyone comes in.

It doesn't look like anything special from the outside, but that doesn't mean anything, especially when it comes to Sabine. Maybe I shouldn't just assume it's from her, but she's the most likely candidate for sending me unidentifiable mail. I just wish we had return address labels like they do in most other countries, but the Royal Mail doesn't seem to have caught on to their appeal.

I carefully unwrap it, scrunching up the paper. With a flick of my wand, I send it sailing towards the recycling bin.

"Yes," I cheer to myself as it goes in. Even if I used magic to do it, there's still something satisfying about getting it in.

A dull brown box sits in front of me. This has to be the worst pass-the-parcel game I've ever played, hasn't Sabine heard of fun wrapping paper?

The lid pops off with ease, and I look down into the box. Something silver shines out from its depths. My eyebrows knit together in a frown as I reach in and pull out a battered bronze looking kettle.

I set it down next to the box and pull off the tag tied around the handle, already recognising the handwriting.

I thought you might like this.

I blink a couple of times, not completely sure what Sabine is think-ing. It's a pretty teapot, with metal that probably once shone, and engravings that can only have been made by magic. It's got the dull look that metal gets when it's not been polished in too long, but that's nothing that a bit of cleaner won't be able to fix.

What I don't understand is why she

thought I'd want this. It's old, but it can't be *too* old. She comes across interesting ancient artefacts all the time, but she can't just send them home to me. Which means it's probably a five-year-old teapot and nothing more.

But the mystery of the teapot is going to have to wait. My first customers will arrive soon and I need to be ready for them or I'll lose the money it takes to keep this place running and myself fed. I live a comfortable life, but a few bad weeks could change that. I don't want to get a normal job, though I suppose my cousins will give me a job at their bakery if things go really bad for me.

As if sensing the direction of my thoughts, the bell rings and the first set of people walk through the door. It's easy to tell the morning people from the night owls. They're bright and cheery, full of polite small talk, whereas the others are more surly and make me think they might turn into murderers if they don't get their coffee.

I smile and pass takeaway cups over at a maddening pace, every now and again using my wand to reset something or make things go a little quicker. It's going to be much better once the new barista starts, it'll mean I finally get the time to do some of the jobs I've been putting off.

Coffee sloshes over my hand as I pull one of the cups away too quickly and I wince as the skin turns red. I pull a mug down from the shelf and stick it under the coffee spout while grabbing the healing syrup from the shelf. A spell would be better, but I don't really have time to stop and do one. I put a couple of squirts into my mug, and then focus back on my customer while the coffee machine does its thing.

I paste a winning smile on my face and hand the travel mug back to the wolf shifter waiting on the other side of the counter. Not many people take advantage of the discount I offer for using their own travel mug, and it makes me happy when they do. It's one less cup that'll be left on the side of a road, or end up in a landfill.

"Two-sixty please," I ask.

He holds a card up to the machine and it beeps, telling me his money is now in my account.

"Have a good day," I sing-song.

"You too," he replies. He's a nice enough guy, though not very talkative. I wonder if it's something to do with the stigma about wolf shifters and werewolves. Not many people are accepting of the differences between the two, and I imagine for the shifters, it can get very annoying.

I turn to the next customer, a human who glances about nervously.

"Hi, what can I get you?" I ask.

He flinches, almost as if he didn't expect me to speak. Such an odd one.

"Is everyone here like him?" he whispers and gestures to the door.

"I doubt it, not everyone is a morning person," I respond, keeping my smile in place only with a lot of effort on my part. I know what he's *really* trying to ask, and so do the rest of the supernatural customers in the line. "What can I get you?" I ask again, refusing to fall for it.

"Do you have pumpkin spice latte?" His eyes dart back and forth. He's very nervous, I have to wonder what that's all about.

"Of course." I take great pleasure in picking up my wand from behind the counter and using it to summon the pumpkin spice mix from the shelves at the back. Normally, I would go get it, but if this man is going to be funny about supernaturals being in the same place as he is, then I'm going to make a show of it. "I've been told I make the best pumpkin spice in town," I say conversationally. Technically, it's my cousin Hazel who says it, but I'm still going to count it.

"Uh-huh."

My smile turns genuine. Good. He's on the back foot now. I've caught him being prejudiced and he doesn't like it. That's always the case with people like him. It's almost as if they think we don't know about the faction of purists who think we shouldn't be allowed to live in society with them. It truly is ridiculous. Especially as I'm sure they'd hate it if they knew we were all hiding amongst them. But there's nothing that can be done about them except continue as if they don't exist.

I set the coffee machine to produce a shot, before turning to the milky portion of his drink. I grab one of the empty metal jugs and dump a portion of pumpkin spice mix in before topping up with milk. Going through the motions of making a latte soothes the annoyance building within me.

The harsh sound of the machine making bubbles in the milk takes even more of my anger away. It'd be easier if I hadn't lost a friend to the propaganda. Not that she's dead, last I heard, she's living somewhere in Scotland with her husband and three children. But she's been disowned from her family and won't keep in contact with anyone after giving up on her magic and going the human route. I don't even understand how it's possible to do that. My wand is a part of me, and I wouldn't be giving it up for anyone. Not even for someone I loved.

I shake my head, trying to rid myself of the memories of Rita's betrayal. It still stings, even now, but I have to ignore it.

The machine beeps, telling me it's done with the coffee. I knock off the milk frother and add the two together. A sprinkle of nutmeg on top and the man's pumpkin spice is ready to go.

"Three sixty-five, please," I say, handing it over to him.

"But his was only two sixty," he protests.

I keep my smile in place, but it's getting harder by the second with this idiot.

"That's because he ordered an americano with a dash of milk, and got the discount for using his own mug." I point at my price list.

The man looks like he's going to argue more, but then shoves a fiver over the counter to me. It doesn't escape my notice that he makes sure not to touch my hand. I click the buttons on my till and pull out the change to hand to him.

He mutters something under his breath, but I don't catch it. That's probably for the best.

"I hope you don't have to see him again," the next man in line says.

"I'm always happy to see all of my customers," I lie, while looking him up and down. He's smartly dressed, classically handsome, and human all the way.

He chuckles. "I worked my way through university in the service industry, I know how to recognise a fake smile."

I laugh lightly, a little bit of panic brewing inside me. I don't want him to be able to tell I'm lying. That makes me all kinds of uncomfortable. "What can I get you?"

"Just an Earl Grey tea, please?"

"Coming right up." I'm glad to get away from him. His piercing gaze is almost as unsettling as the other man's supernaturalphobia.

Once I've handed the man his tea, the rest of the morning rush goes by without a hitch. People don't talk to me more than they have to, meaning all I have to say are the necessary pleasantries that make the world go around. Even so, the strange events of the morning confuse me. It's going to be an odd day, I can feel it in my bones.

Chapter 2

I blow across the top of my coffee before taking a sip. I used to be a tea drinker, but then Grandpa opened my eyes to the wonders of coffee. He used to travel a lot and always brought me back a bag of the best coffee he could find from wherever he'd been. Once I was old enough, he'd take me with him.

I glance at the photo of him hanging behind the coffee shop counter, a familiar combination of bittersweet happiness spreading through me. I wish he'd been alive to see me open Cauldron Coffee Shop, he'd have loved it.

At least I can rest while the coffee shop is quiet. There are a couple of students from the nearby academy settled into one of the corner booths, and the odd person will pop in for a drink and maybe a slice of cake, but this is the quiet time and I know better than to waste it. There's always an ebb and flow to running a coffee shop. It'll get busy again around four, and then again when the vampires surface to start their days after sundown.

I only stay open late for them. I tried doing early mornings too, but they seem to be more focused on getting home than anything else. Which makes sense to me. If the sun could burn me to a crisp, I'd want to be home with the blackout blinds drawn well in advance of sunrise.

I shudder at the thought, relieved to be a witch and not a vampire. Not for the first time either, I heard enough horror stories from the vampires studying at Grimalkin Academy while I was there. I'm not sure how they manage to get through their days. Most of them are used to it, I'm sure, especially with turning being illegal in all but a few cases. If it doesn't save someone's life, and the person hasn't consented, then the vamps can't turn them.

Luckily for me, the witch laws are a lot less strict. Not that I have the ability to turn a human into a magical being anyway.

The shrill ring of the phone makes me jump and I scramble to answer it. At least the students in the corner aren't paying much attention and don't see me make a fool out of myself. But it's important that I pick up. Not many people have this line, and most of them are suppliers, I can't miss a call.

"Good Afternoon, how can I help you?" I say, sounding as cheery and polished as I can and not like I've just almost ended up flat on my face.

"Willow is that you?"

"Sabine?" Why is she calling the landline instead of my mobile?

"Yes, of course it's me, don't you recognise my voice?" She chuckles, taking any sting there is out of her words.

"You just called my coffee shop and were surprised I answered," I point out.

"You might have finally done what I suggested and gotten yourself a member of staff," she counters. "You haven't though, have you?"

"Actually, I have."

She gasps dramatically. "Who are you and what have you done with my best friend?"

I let out a low chuckle, knowing she's only jesting. "I haven't done anything. I just realised that maybe you were right and I should listen to you."

"Now I think you've been possessed. Do I need to get one of the local reapers to come visit and check for ghosts?"

I shake my head in amusement

even though she can't see me. "You realise I'd be able to see the ghost too, right?"

"Hmm. Maybe you banged your head and lost the ability."

"Everyone has the ability." Supernaturals more than humans, which explains how reapers were able to keep ghosts a secret until recently.

"But a knock to the head might explain why you're listening to my advice now."

"I've listened to your advice for years," I point out. "Remember the time I nearly turned Eddie Draymond into a frog?"

"You would have gotten into so much trouble if you'd gone through with that."

"And I didn't, thanks to you. Now, I always think twice before I turn people into frogs."

"You're such a stereotypical witch," she jokes.

"And you owe me an explanation for the teapot you sent," I counter, bringing us back to what she actually called about.

I glance at the front door, making sure I haven't suddenly had a customer appear. That would be just my luck.

Her tinkling laugh comes down the line. "It arrived then?"

"This morning, but you know that." The chances of Sabine not bothering to track a parcel are next to none. She's always careful, and as an archaeologist, she has the ability to do it fairly easily.

"I do," she admits. "But you might not have opened it."

"In which case, you'd be calling to get me to do that while you're on the line."

Sabine lets out a satisfied sigh. "You know me so well."

"I've lived with you for too long then."

"So, the teapot..." she prompts.

I immediately look at the pot, noticing it shining in the sunlight. I reach out to touch it, trailing my finger down the intricate pattern.

"Where's it from?" I ask.

There's silence down the line that makes me worry about what Sabine has done to get hold of this. "I had to send it to you," she says after a moment.

"Had to?"

"Mmhmm. You'll understand in a few days."

I frown, confused by what she means, but not questioning it too much. I trust her, she's not going to have sent anything dangerous to my house.

I hope.

"How will I understand?" I ask, more curious than anything else.

Sabine sighs. "I'm not sure. I can't explain it, but when I picked up the teapot, I could feel that it wanted me to send it to you."

"Maybe the teapot is the possessed one," I mutter.

Something akin to affirmation radiates off the item in question.

I frown, wondering if I'm imagining it just because it's what I'm thinking about. I shake my head to rid myself of the thoughts. I can't let a teapot drive me crazy or I won't last another week in the coffee shop business.

"It isn't haunted, the reaper on staff said there was no ghost." She doesn't add that as a necromancer, she'd be able to tell if it contained the ghost of a supernatural, but the implication is there. She just doesn't want to say what she is in case anyone is listening in that shouldn't be. The world isn't always kind to necromancers, even when it should be.

"I'll take your word for it." Especially because I'm not about to walk into the local Reaper Guard quarters and ask them to take a look at my teapot because there might be a ghost in it. They'd laugh me out of the building.

"I'm coming home next week," she says.

I let out a loud squeak. "You are?"

Even with being thousands of miles away from me, I can almost see her smiling.

"I am," she assures me. "I got asked to lead an excavation of the Humber Stone, so I'll be coming home next weekend."

"Isn't that a little bit outside your expertise?"

She sighs. "Don't get me started, but it's good money and a reason to visit you and my family. That's enough for me."

"Then I'm glad. I can't wait to see you. I'll make sure your room is ready." I doubt the sheets will still be fresh after months spent unused.

"Thanks, I did think about booking a hotel and just stopping by, but I changed my mind."

"I'm glad to hear it. If you weren't going to, then I might be forced to revoke your status as my best friend."

She makes a fake shocked noise. "After all these years and the beautiful teapot I just sent you?"

"That depends if the teapot really is haunted."

"Mmhmm. I see where we stand," she jokes.

"I'm really looking forward to seeing you," I say more seriously.

"Me too. It's been too long."

The bell at the front of the shop tinkles, announcing a new customer. "I have to go, message me?"

"Always."

I hang up the phone and turn my attention to my new customer, a wide smile on my face that's completely genuine. I always love it when I get to see my best friend, I miss her when she's not around, even if I know it's good for her career not to stay here.

My gaze slips to the teapot. Something about it is strangely captivating, even if I can't fully explain what it is. Maybe once the day is over, I'll be able to get to the bottom of what is so strange about it.

Chapter 3

I yawn and rub my eyes as I make my way down into the coffee shop. I like mornings, but sometimes sleep is still hard to shake.

"Meow."

I stop in my tracks. "Spooky?" I call out, already knowing who the owner of the feline voice is.

I step into the coffee shop to find the tortoiseshell cat perching on the counter next to the teapot, almost looking as if she's deep in conversation with it.

"You're going to have to tell me who your owner is one of these days," I mutter, making my way over to the cat despite my stern tone.

Something like disapproval comes off the teapot in waves.

"I was talking to Spooky, not you." I pat the cat on the head, gaining a few purrs for my trouble. I've no idea where she normally lives, just that she likes to make herself comfortable in my coffee shop from time to time. I don't even know how she manages to get into the building either.

But despite knowing it creates extra cleaning, I can't help but indulge her. I know what cats are like, if this is the place she wants to hang out, then that's what she's going to do.

"You're going to have to get off the counter," I tell her. "Customers will be arriving soon."

She lets out a slightly indignant sound, but jumps off anyway.

I pick up the spray and a clean cloth and set about cleaning the various surfaces she could have been on.

"Sorry, I need to move you," I say to the teapot as I lift it up and set it on the shelf above the till.

A sense of understanding drifts from it, but I'm pretty sure I'm imagining it.

I have to be. Teapots don't have feelings.

I continue setting up for the day without any interruptions from the cat or the pot, though both are still present in my near vicinity. It seems that my coffee shop is becoming more of a guest house by the day.

The first few customers of the day go without a hitch, which isn't a surprise. Most of them are regulars who never change their orders, which makes it very easy to have everything ready.

But this isn't an ordinary day. My new barista is coming in at ten and I don't know whether to be excited or worried about it. I've never had anyone work for me before and it's going to be a different experience for me.

"Hey," a handsome man in a neat suit says.

I do a quick scan of him to make sure I don't recognise him, and put on a winning smile. "Good morning, welcome to Cauldron Coffee Shop, what can I get for you?"

"What's good?"

"I'd be a bad owner if I didn't say that everything was," I respond.

He chuckles. "So you're as intelligent as you are beautiful?"

A flush rises to my cheeks despite the fact I know not to be too flattered by customers flirting with me, it's just part of the job. "Do you prefer tea or coffee?" I ask, trying to keep professional.

"Coffee."

"I can do everything from a plain black coffee, to something with a bit more zing."

"Can anything here be called plain?"

Disapproval comes in waves from the shelf holding the teapot, and it takes everything I have to ignore it. I don't need a teapot telling me how to handle my life.

"Do you need a shot of anything? We have classic syrups like hazelnut and peppermint, but we also have magical ones. Alertness is particularly popular at the moment." The clocks have just changed and everyone wants to make sure that they're on the ball for their morning meetings.

"Alertness sounds good," he says, finally backing off with the flirting. "What does that go well with?"

"Cappuccino," I answer instantly. I've tried all the possible combinations so I can make the best suggestions to customers.

"Then that sounds perfect."

"Great." I smile at him and start making his drink, thankful that he seems to have stopped with the flirting.

Once he's served, I move on to the next customer, repeating the process and the conversations over and over. At some point, Spooky disappears, either back to where she actually lives, or to find somewhere to bask in the morning sun. Somehow, I suspect it's the latter.

Every now and again, I glance at the teapot to check it hasn't done something strange like sprout arms and legs. I'm certain that I felt emotions coming off it, but that doesn't actually make sense.

Teapots don't get jealous. It's as simple as that.

"Hey," the next customer says.

I look up to find my new barista standing on the other side of the counter. Is it that time already? Somehow the hours have slipped by without me noticing much. I'm not even sure how that's possible.

"Morning," I say. "Why don't we sit down and I'll take you through the basics." I gesture to my normal table.

She nods and makes her way over, setting her bag on the floor.

"Do you want anything to drink?"
She shakes her head.

"All right then." I grab the stack of

papers I printed off earlier for her to fill in, along with the name tag I had made.

Aisha. It suits her.

I grab my half-drunk coffee and go to sit down opposite her. "I hope you don't mind if I have one, it's been a long morning already."

"Is it always busy first thing?"

"On weekdays, yes. Weekends tend to be quieter in the mornings, but steadier throughout the day. You'll get used to it." Though maybe she won't need to, I mostly plan on scheduling her for when I know it's going to be busy and I could do with another pair of hands. "Do you have any questions for me?" I don't think I'm doing the whole new starter process right, but so long as she gets the information she needs, that's the main thing.

"Where did you get that teapot?" she asks, nodding towards the shelf where Sabine's present sits.

I try to cover my surprise that it's what she's asking about. "It was a gift from a friend," I respond. "Why do you ask?"

"Sorry, I didn't mean to pry, it just looked familiar to me."

"It's okay, I'd always rather you asked." I smile reassuringly at her, only to be nudged by a sense of unease that I'm pretty sure is coming from the teapot.

I really need to let it stop affecting me this much. It's just an old teapot that I know next to nothing about. Hopefully, Sabine will answer more of my questions about it when she turns up next week.

"Anyway, here are the forms I need you to fill in. Just standard stuff so I can make sure I have the right insurance and can pay you." I set it all down in front of you. "Take your time, I brought you in between rushes so that you can get to know the coffee shop more easily."

"Thank you," Aisha responds. "I appreciate it."

I nod. "I'm just going to go and

catch up on some of the washing up, but I'm right here if you need anything."

"Thanks."

I head back behind the counter, resisting the urge to grab the teapot and squirrel it away somewhere else. I'm not completely certain that the thoughts are even coming from me. Whatever the truth is behind the pot, it's more complicated than anything I've ever encountered before.

Chapter 4

I hum to myself as I clean down the surfaces, enjoying the peace and tranquillity of the coffee shop at this time.

"I'll see you later, Willow," Aisha says, waving at me as she leaves after her shift.

"See you later," I respond with a wave of my own. She's doing well so far, even if I still end up feeling uneasy whenever she's around the teapot.

She doesn't linger, leaving me alone, even if it's probably not going to be for long.

As if summoned by my thoughts, the bell rings and someone steps inside.

I glance up ready to greet them, only to be stopped in my tracks by the dark-haired necromancer who has just stepped into my shop.

"Sabine!" I hurry over to her and throw my arms around my best friend, hugging her tightly.

She wraps her arms around me and returns the embrace, as I knew she would. I don't hug many people, but I always hug her.

"I wasn't expecting you until the weekend," I say as I pull back, looking her up and down. "Did you need something?"

She chuckles uncomfortably. "If I say yes, is that bad?"

"I'd expect nothing less. But you'll have to pay the toll if you want help," I tease good-naturedly. She knows I'll help even without it.

"Oh? And what is that?"

"You can tell me about the teapot." I gesture to the pot sitting on the side. I always think that I'm not going to put it so prominently on display, but then I do it anyway, I don't even know why half of the time.

"I don't have any explanation," she admits. "It's almost like it made me do things."

I stare at the pot for a moment longer than necessary and then nod. "I get that. It makes me take it upstairs with me at the end of the day. I think it's alive."

Alarm flits over Sabine's face, as if she's worried about something more than a teapot with emotions. "And how are you feeling? You're not extra tired? Hungrier than normal? Craving something you don't normally..."

"Sabine," I cut her off sharply, knowing it's the only way to stop her from spiralling. "I'm fine. You don't have to worry about me."

"But the teapot..."

"Is friendly," I finish, not realising I feel that way until the words are out of my mouth. But they're true. I'm convinced the teapot is friendly, even if I'm not sure why.

Sabine raises an eyebrow, but doesn't say anything.

I ponder adding to my comment for a minute, but decide against it, heading behind the counter instead so I can make her one of her favourite drinks. We've known each other for so long that I don't need to ask what she wants.

I drop the ingredients into the blender and stick it in the machine that'll turn it into an iced frappé.

"You're looking well. Did you manage to recharge on a pile of old bones or something?" I ask as I slide the coffee over.

"Thanks," she says as she takes it. "And it was a mummy, you know bones don't do much."

A shiver runs down my spine. I know that she has to use the dead to recharge, but I still find it strange. "It's weird that's what you do."

"I don't have any control over how I have to recharge my magic," she points out. "I'm not like you with an endless supply fuelled by nothing. I have to be around death. This is just less creepy than hanging around a hospital."

"You're not wrong there," I mutter, trying not to think about the kind of person who would do that. "Though I still haven't *seen* any necromancers doing that."

"How much time are you spending at the hospital?"

"Barely any, especially since I broke it off with the doctor." Even then, we spent more time in bed than at the hospital.

A rattle comes from the direction of the teapot, drawing our attention to it.

"Does it do that often?" Sabine asks.

I shrug. "Sometimes, I think it's jealous."

"How can a teapot be jealous?"

"How can a lot of things be the case," I counter, realising I've become a little more used to the teapot's feelings. I thought I'd be more annoyed at it, but now Sabine is questioning things, I want to defend it instead. "It just is."

"I can find someone to take it off you if you want..."

"No need," I cut her off quickly without realising what I'm doing. "I like the company. I know that sounds weird."

"I've known you were weird for at least ten years."

"True. And now you're stuck with me. They say if a friendship lasts seven years then it's going to be for life," I respond. "Are you staying here every night?"

She nods. "The dig is only about an hour away."

"I know, I checked it on the map. It's nice for you to be so close to home for a change. How was the site?"

"About what you'd expect, it's a big green field with a stone in the middle of it."

"That sounds riveting." I make my

way around so I can sit with her in the comfy chairs to the side of the counter.

"Mmmhmm." She takes a sip of her coffee.

"I found a product online that might appeal to any necromancer customers I might get. Do you mind if I order some and test it on you?" If I'd have thought about it, I'd have asked her and ordered it before she arrived.

Sabine glances around the coffee shop, probably to check that there aren't any other customers that can hear our conversation about what she is.

"I can, but I don't think they'll be ordering it," she reminds me.

But I've thought this through, and don't plan on having them order anything that will out their necromancer status. "I wouldn't have them order a coffee with death or anything obvious like that. They'd come and ask me for my famous spiderweb latte."

"Please tell me it doesn't include

actual spiders." She shudders dramatically.

"For someone who spends a lot of time in old abandoned buildings, it's surprising you hate spiders as much as you do." I'm pretty sure she deals with them on a daily basis when she's at a dig site.

"I can't help it."

"There are no spiders," I promise.

"Then I'll try it, but I can't promise anything about necromancers coming in."

I shrug. "That's fine. I just don't want them thinking I'm excluding them. I want everyone to know they're welcome here." It's one of the things I promised myself when I set up the coffee shop with the inheritance from Grandpa. I want to make sure every-one, supernatural and human alike, can find something for them on the menu.

Sabine smiles at me in a way that makes me certain she's touched by my thoughts of her people. Necromancers are secretive by nature, even since supernaturals came out in the open. And with good reason. Vampires hate them because they can be used as necromancer food. Which is ironic when they need blood in order to survive, but maybe that's what makes them so squeamish about it.

"So, you were telling me about the dig site," I prompt, wanting to change the subject to one she'll be more comfortable with.

"Oh, right. The most interesting thing is probably that Sawyer was there."

"What?" The question comes out as more of a high-pitched squeal. I didn't expect her to come in and tell me that her ex-boyfriend is at her dig site. "You talked about spiders and didn't lead with that? What was he doing there? *Please* tell me he was there to beg for you back?"

"Not even slightly. He was there for the Department of Magical Heritage."

She sounds slightly amused for reasons I'm not really sure about.

"Oh eesh, that's not good." I'm not even in her field and I know that the DMH can cause a lot of trouble, particularly if they think the person in charge of the dig site isn't doing their job properly.

"It's not bad either. He wants me to stop the excavation, but the DMH has already approved it."

"That sounds like quite the quandary."

"For him, yes. For me, not so much. My dig will continue as planned." There's a hint of smugness in her voice, which is probably just from the thought of thwarting Sawyer's plans.

"Is he going to keep hanging around?" I ask.

She shrugs. "No idea."

"Just...be careful if he does." I don't want to see her heart broken again.

Her eyebrows shoot up and a disbelieving expression crosses her face.

"Don't look at me like that. I want

whatever you want for yourself. That's my job as best friend."

"Hmm."

"I liked Sawyer, and he was good for you while you were together. But if he's not good for you now, then I don't support it." And it's as simple as that as far as I'm concerned. Sawyer is a good guy, but that doesn't mean he's the right guy for her.

It doesn't mean he's the wrong one either.

"Thanks, Willow."

"Just trust yourself. Your heart will lead you in the right direction," I promise, meaning every word.

"I hope you're right."

"I normally am." Something she's well aware of.

Sabine lets out a soft groan and pulls out her phone. Even from her expression, I can tell it's not good.

"Bad news?" I ask.

"They need me back at the dig site."

"But you'll be home tonight, right?"

I hope so. I want to spend more time with her.

She nods.

"Great, I'll have your bed made up for you." Thankfully, I already washed her sheets, I just need to actually put them on the bed.

"Thanks." She sets down her iced coffee mug and gets to her feet, heading towards the door.

"I'll see you in a bit," I call to her.

"Bye!" she shouts back.

I sigh and lean back in my chair, grateful that I get extra time with my best friend, even if it's not going to be for too long.

Chapter 5

I pick up my pumpkin spice latte and take a sip, enjoying the taste and the slight zing of energy I get from the magical shot. I don't often put one in, but sometimes when I'm closing up the shop, a little extra isn't a bad thing.

Spooky jumps up onto the counter and meows loudly at the teapot sitting on the shelf.

The sudden desire to move the pot to sit next to her goes through me, and I move without thinking, picking it up and setting it down again.

"Better?" I ask the pot.

Affirmation comes from it,

reminding me of how used to the whole situation I've become. When the teapot arrived, I'd never have been able to guess that I'd end up talking to it this much. At least Sabine won't be home for another few hours, which means I don't have to answer all of her questions about it. Not that she should be asking when she's the one who got me into this predicament in the first place.

I take another sip of coffee and then put my mug onto the counter next to the two of them.

I sigh. It's been a long day, and I'm looking forward to heading upstairs and turning in for the night. I love my job, and the coffee shop is everything I've ever wanted, but that doesn't mean I don't get exhausted sometimes.

An empty bottle of syrup clutters up the side. I turn and grab it, tossing it in the recycling box. Though I'm dreading having to take it outside, I know I have to. Maybe I should schedule Aisha to work an evening shift at some point soon so I can actually get some rest.

Is that too mean?

It's hard to tell, I've never actually been a boss before.

"Meow."

I frown. Is it me, or is Spooky sounding perplexed? First the teapot, now the cat, I seem to be pushing complex emotions onto everything I can think of and I need to stop before I end up going through some kind of psyche evaluation and lose my wand over it. That's never going to be a good thing.

I carry on tidying up, trying to ignore the slight unease building inside me. I'm not sure where it's coming from, or what's going on, but something big is about to happen, I can feel it in my bones.

"Meow."

This time, Spooky's call is followed by a wet splash and a loud crack.

I whirl around in time to find the teapot lying in a pool of coffee, shards of broken mug scattered around it, and a smug-looking cat licking her paws with a nonchalance that suggests she doesn't want any of the blame.

"Why did you do that?" I ask the cat, having no doubt she's the one responsible for this mess. She hasn't done anything like it before, which is just adding to the strangeness of the situation.

She stops licking her paw and lifts her head so her gaze can meet mine.

Unsurprisingly, I don't find any answers in it.

"Step back, I'll clean it up," I say, shooing her with one hand while reaching for my wand with the other. Thankfully, a quick cleaning spell should be all that's needed in order to put this right.

I clear my throat even though I don't actually need to say anything, and wave my wand in the direction of the counter. Tingles shoot up and down my arm as my magic surges forth. I funnel all my will into it, telling the mess on the counter to retake the forms they normally have.

The mug starts to piece itself back together and the coffee sloshes back inside. Not that I plan on drinking it once it's there. After a few mishaps, it's easy to learn that some things are best left untouched even if they're fixed with magic.

The teapot rights itself and starts to shudder.

My eyes widen and I step back. A quick glance at Spooky reveals that she's very unaffected by the situation and has turned her attention back to her paw. Either she has no idea what's going on, or it's not as bad as I fear it's going to be.

I'm not sure which I want to be the case.

A large puff of maroon smoke fills the air, stinging my eyes and tickling the back of my throat. I cough a couple of times to clear it, wishing I'd known what was about to happen so I could have kept my mouth shut.

I wave away the smoke, not daring to use magic to make it go away. Using a spell on something that's clearly been activated by magic is never a good idea, every parent teaches their young witch not to do it, and with good reason. That's often how curses end up formed.

After a moment, the smoke finally begins to clear and my shock deepens as I stare at the man standing in front of me.

No, not standing.

Floating.

He's *floating* in front of me.

"Hello?" My voice shakes, which probably isn't surprising given the unexpected guest in my coffee shop. "Can I help you?"

The man's gaze flits around the room, taking it in as if it's the first time he's seeing it. Which makes sense, I'm sure he has no idea how he got here. To be fair, I have no idea how he got here either.

He starts to speak, his words

coming thick and fast in a language I don't understand. I vaguely recognise it, but not well enough to actually work out what it is.

"Whoa," I say, holding up my hands. "Slow down. What language are you speaking? I can do a translation spell?" I repeat the same question in French and German. He's not speaking either of them, but they're the only other languages I know, hopefully he does too.

The man pauses and studies me, as if he's trying to decide what to say next. "I am in England," he says slowly in accented English.

I nod. "You are."

"Ah, my apologies, last I knew, I was in Egypt," he says.

I blink a couple of times. That's where Sabine's dig was, is he suggesting that he somehow came here in the teapot.

My gaze slips to it, but I can't tell if it looks any different to how it did before. I don't think it does.

The man follows my gaze and nods grimly. "Yes. The teapot is my home."

"You know that raises more questions than it answers, right?" Should I be freaking out more than I am? I've never been in this situation before, though from the sounds of it, he might have been.

"I apologise, I should have started with an introduction. I am Azíl," he says proudly.

"Willow," I respond, a little less sure than he seems to be. I just want to know answers to some of the more obvious questions. Like who is he, and what's he doing in my coffee shop. Though I suppose technically, he's answered the first one by giving me his name.

Which makes this all the more complicated.

"How did you get here?" I ask.

"You put me there." He waves to the counter where the teapot is sitting.

I sigh. "I know that. How did you get *here*." I gesture to the wider coffee shop, though that's not even really my question either. Mostly, I want to know how he got into the teapot in the first place, and how he ended up sent to me.

"It is a long story," Azíl responds.

"I can make time for it," I mutter. "Look, why don't I make us some coffee, and then you can tell me?"

Surprise flits over his face, as if he didn't expect me to offer him a drink.

Wait, can he drink? I glance down at the slightly transparent view of his legs and find myself questioning that.

"That sounds agreeable," he responds.

I sigh with relief and set about making two black coffees. I need something strong, and he doesn't feel like he's ready for anything fancy.

How have I ended up in this situation?

I bet it's Sabine's fault.

Chapter 6

Azíl sits in the comfortable looking chair opposite me, cupping his mug in his hand and staring at it like it's the best thing he's ever been offered.

Have I accidentally done something wrong? I'm not sure.

"Thank you for the coffee," he says. "You are the first person I have appeared before who has actually offered me any."

I frown. "You've appeared in front of more people before?"

He nods. "You do not think you are the first person I have appeared to in three thousand years, do you?"

My eyes widen.

Three. Thousand. Years. Is that how old he is?

"You've been trapped in a teapot for three thousand years?" I ask, trying to work it out in my head.

"Unfortunately, yes."

"Are you a genie?"

"Do I look like a genie?"

I cross my arms and give him a stern look. "If you didn't look like a genie, would I be asking if you were one?"

"Have you ever met a genie?"

"No."

"Then how do you know I look like one?"

Why is he so infuriating? Is this what living in a teapot for several thousand years does to someone? I'll have to make a note never to get myself into a predicament like this.

"I'm just a warlock," he says. "A powerful one, but a warlock all the same."

"Warlocks don't live for thousands of years."

"They do if they live in a teapot," he mutters.

"How did that happen? Did you connect yourself to it on purpose?"

"I am not a fool."

I shrug. "I'm not suggesting you are. People have done weirder things in the search for immortality."

"Hmm. That is fair. I knew a man who slept with his feet wrapped in palm leaves because he thought it would extend his life."

"Did it work?"

"Not even slightly. He died when he was twenty-five."

I resist the urge to laugh at his matter-of-fact tone.

"So how did you end up in the teapot?"

"That is not a story for now." He glances away, and if I had to guess, I'd say there's a small hint of embarrass-ment in his eyes.

That's fine. I can wait for the story of how he became trapped in the teapot. I have more important things to ask anyway.

"What made you appear here today?" I ask. "Your pot has been here for nearly two weeks, why not before?"

"You used a spell to free me."

I frown. "I don't think I did."

He shrugs. "You must have, because I am here, and that is the only way to let me out temporarily. I can not release myself, no matter for how short an amount of time."

"So if you go back in, you can't come out again?"

"Actually, no," he acknowledges. "Now you have let me out once, I can come and go as I please so long as the teapot is beside me, unless you plan on binding me closer to the teapot." He takes a sip of his coffee.

"You don't seem very worried that I'll do that."

"I am not," he agrees. "You feel like a good person."

"You barely know me."

"I have known you for nearly two weeks," he points out. "We may not have had conversations with one another, but I have been there, watching, listening, and getting to know who you are in your soul."

"You have to know how creepy that sounds," I mutter.

"I apologise, I do not intend to make you feel that way."

"There's no need," I say quickly. "I've not felt that way about you or your teapot." I take a sip of my coffee.

He nods as if I've understood something fundamental about the situation.

"I did not expect you to look so beautiful," he says.

I choke on my drink. "Sorry," I murmur. "You can't just say that to people."

"Why not? It is a compliment, is it not?"

"It is. But you can't go around saying it."

"Even to beautiful women?"

"Especially to beautiful women."

He sighs dramatically. "It seems the world has changed once again since the last time I was freed from my prison."

"When was that?" I ask, mostly out of curiosity, but partly so I can know what to expect from him when he says things.

"I think it was nineteen-twenty-two."

"In Egypt?" I check.

He nods. "Though I originally knew the land as Kemet."

I study him intently, trying to decide if he's pulling my leg about being stuck in a teapot for three thousand years. Somehow, I want to believe him, and I'm not exactly sure why. Something about him feels trustworthy.

"Is that where you're from? Before all of this." The teapot doesn't look very Egyptian in style, but that doesn't mean anything. Maybe he picked it for other reasons.

"No. My country did not have a

name at the time, but I believe you now call it Morocco."

"You're very up to date on current affairs to say you claim to have been living in a teapot for thousands of years." I set down my empty mug and lean back in my chair. It's not that I don't believe him, there are just a lot of potential holes in his story and I want to make sure I correctly get to the bottom of them.

"The last person who let me out was a great scholar. I helped him understand what I knew of the secrets of Kemet, he helped me understand the modern world. Though I suppose to you, the world he taught me about no longer exists."

"I don't think you're doing too badly on getting it right," I assure him. "Is he how you learned English?"

Azíl nods. "He was a very strict teacher, but I believe it has paid off."

"It has. You're very good."

His lips quirk up into an amused smile, only serving to draw my attention to how pleasant he is to look at. I'm not sure whether it's the neatly groomed beard, or the twinkle in his eyes that speaks of innocent mischief, but there's something almost enchanting about him.

"So what happens now?" I ask. "You're not in your teapot." Though he has brought it with him.

"I suppose that depends if you are planning on trapping me in it again."

"I'm not. But would I admit that if I was going to?"

"I already know you will not," he responds. "I could sense the kind of person you were when you were carrying my teapot around. And you talked to me. Not everyone does that."

"Oh, well, I guess I could kind of feel your emotions through it," I admit.

"I thought as much. I am glad that you did. It has been a long time since I talked with someone. I enjoyed it."

"I'm glad." I smile at him, somehow completely at ease despite the fact he hasn't said anything about why he lived in a teapot for three thousand years. Some of what he's saying makes it seem as if it wasn't entirely voluntary, which only piques my interest more.

But I shouldn't press him past his comfort zone just because I want to know the answers. It doesn't sound like he's going anywhere, there'll be time for me to learn them.

"Where is the cat?" he asks, glancing around. "I want to thank her for helping you release me."

"Spooky? She's probably gone home. She doesn't live here."

"Ah. She likes the name you have given her."

My eyebrows shoot up. "You can speak cat?"

Azíl chuckles, a deep rich sound that fills me with warmth. "No. But when you have spent as much time as an inanimate object as I have, you learn to read the things people do not say out loud. That includes animals. She likes you."

"Oh. I'm glad. Though maybe her current owners won't be as pleased about that."

"Cats will do what cats are going to do."

"That's very true," I agree. "I've never known a cat who doesn't have a mind of its own."

"I have seen many things change, but cats never do," Azíl says as he sets his empty mug down on the table between us.

"I don't think they ever will."

"Perhaps not. Thank you for the coffee, it was delightful."

"How have you been eating and drinking in the teapot?" I blurt. "Is there food in there?"

He chuckles. "There is not. I do not have to eat and drink, but I can choose to if I want to."

"Oh. So you haven't eaten much in the past three thousand years?" Maybe he is a genie, but just in denial about it. Is that even possible? I don't know much about them, but a little research will sort that out.

"Only the occasional thing here and there when the people who freed me weren't looking."

I frown. "None of them offered you anything, ever?"

"They probably thought I did not need it."

"Everyone needs kindness," I point out.

"Perhaps."

"What's your favourite food?" The question bursts from me. "I mean, I can order some for you if I can get hold of it, but I need to know what you like."

"Sweet things," he admits. "Particularly flavoured with honey. Or dates. But I am sure there are many things in your modern world that I may like."

I'm going to find him his new favourite food. I'm not sure why it matters so much to me, but I'm going to ignore the little voice in my head telling me that I'm being an idiot. Perhaps I shouldn't be trusting the random warlock who is claiming crazy things about living in a teapot, but something about him convinces me it's true, and it's not just his attachment to the pot either.

I pull out my phone and dash a quick message off to Clover. I don't normally stock my cousin's baklava in the coffee shop like I do with her sisters' biscuits and cakes, but if Azíl likes sweet honey flavoured things, then it's the perfect choice, and I know she'll set some aside for me. Or, if I'm lucky, she'll bring it by so I don't have to do anything.

I set my phone down and smile at my unexpected guest. "So, what happens now? Are you staying out of the teapot for good? I have a guest room upstairs that I can make up for you." I can't believe I'm offering it to him. On the other hand, I can. He's been living in the flat and coffee shop as a teapot for almost two weeks, if anything bad was going to happen, it would have already.

He shakes his head. "I will be content inside the pot."

"You want to go back inside there?" It still isn't clear whether he's been living in the teapot by choice, or if it's something more sinister than that, but it doesn't sit well with me.

"Some things become comforting over time. There is a lot of open space that I am no longer used to. But if it is acceptable to you, I wish to come out of the teapot when we are alone."

"Of course. I'd like that." And I mean it. He's been easy to talk to, and I don't want him to feel alone now that I know he's in there. "I can bring your teapot down to the coffee shop with me each morning if you'd like to, then you can watch what goes on."

"I cannot see while I am in the pot," he says. "But I would still like that. I can sense the world around me, and it makes me feel less alone."

"I hope that I can help with that."

"You already have," he assures me. "And for that, I will be eternally grateful." A sadness enters his voice that reveals more than he thinks it does.

And that makes me determined to find a way to make sure he doesn't spend the next three thousand years of his life in a teapot.

Chapter 7

The babble of dozens of voices fills the coffee shop, and the display case is looking rather empty with all the cakes I've sold. It's a good job Clover said she'd drop by later, because I'm going to need more than just baklava from my cousins.

I glance at the teapot sitting on the shelf above the till and smile at it. I should feel weird about knowing Azíl is sitting inside and observing everything, but I don't.

He's comforting to have around, and I'm not even sure why.

A new customer approaches the till

and I take a deep breath, readying myself for their order.

"Good afternoon, welcome to Cauldron Coffee Shop, what can I get for you?" I ask brightly.

"Just a coffee to go, no extras," the woman responds, giving nothing away.

"Of course, coming right up." I turn to grab an empty takeaway cup, keeping half an eye on her as I work. I'm not sure what it is about her, but something feels a little off.

I push the thought aside. It's probably just to do with whatever inherent magic she might have. I can't tell just from her presence, which is a little unusual, but not unheard of. The only reason I'm able to tell for most people is because of years in the service industry. It's easy to pick up that someone's a werewolf when they come in and order a shot of calm every few hours around the full moon.

Not that I ever question them about it. I just put on a smile on my face and go about the rest of my day as if I know nothing about any of it.

I quickly put together a cup of coffee, only stopping to glance in Azíl's direction to check he's okay.

Something about the current situation feels strange, and I don't know what it is. I focus hard to try and sense if there are any emotions coming from the pot, but don't pick up on anything. Maybe it's different now that he's been able to break free.

"Here you go," I say to the woman as I set the sealed takeaway cup on the counter in front of her. "That'll be two-seventy, please."

She gives me a tight smile and lifts her card to signal how she'd like to pay. I press a button on the till so the machine will light up.

"That's a lovely teapot," she says as she waves her card over the screen. It beeps, signalling that her payment has gone through.

I barely look away from her to check on Azíl. "Thank you."

"Where did you get it from?" she asks.

"It was a gift."

A sense of unease comes from the shelf. Or maybe from me. I don't know what's happening, but something about the situation doesn't feel right, and I'm not sure exactly what it is.

"Ah, such an interesting gift." She gives me a tight smile. "Thank you for the coffee." She starts to head towards the door, only to stop and start talking to Aisha who has been clearing tables as people leave.

There are a few hand gestures, and what looks to be quite an intense conversation, but I'm not sure what it's about. Aisha is probably just doing her job and being friendly to the customer, it's what I'm paying her for.

I sigh and turn away, looking towards Azíl. Well, towards his teapot. Technically, I know they're two separate things, but I'm viewing them a little bit like one at the moment. Perhaps it'll change with time.

"Am I right in thinking that's weird?" I ask him.

Affirmation comes from the pot.

"Hmm." I'm just getting suspicious in my old age, but I don't think so. The only other person who has shown interest in the pot so far is Aisha, but that's understandable when she's working here.

Maybe the woman could sense that there's a soul inside the pot. Some supernaturals can do things like that, so it could be an explanation. Anyone would be interested in it if they could sense Azíl's emotions coming from it.

How have I gotten myself in this situation again?

Oh, right, it's Sabine's fault. I'll have to think of a suitable penalty for her.

The door to the coffee shop opens, and I'm about to ready myself for a new customer when I realise it's just Clover armed with a few boxes of cakes for me.

"They let you off counter duty," I

joke with my cousin once she gets to me. She's almost always the one who does the actual selling at Broomstick Bakery, while her three sisters do the baking in the back. Mostly because Clover's speciality comes in the form of drenched, but keepable, baklava.

She chuckles. "Hazel's taken over while she's waiting for her macarons to rest before she bakes them."

"I'm going to have to nod and pretend I know what it takes to make macarons."

Clover lets out a light laugh. "You and me both. You'd have thought she was a witch from the way she puts those things together. Oh wait..."

Amusement fills me at our childhood joke. It's probably not funny to anyone else, but the five of us always found it hilarious to say we were like witches when it's what we actually are.

"Do you want a coffee?"

"A chai tea, if you don't mind. I'm trying to cut back on caffeine."

"You realise there's caffeine in tea

too, right?" I pull out a takeaway cup and start making her one as we talk.

"I said cut back, not completely stop with it. That sounds horrendous." She gives an exaggerated shudder.

"Coming right up. Do you want a shot of anything in it?" I ask.

She shakes her head. "I ate one of Oakley's pep-in-your-step brownies earlier on, I don't think it's good to mix magic."

"Probably a good idea."

"She included some in here." She taps the boxes. "She thought your customers might like the pick-me-up."

"Oh, they'll go down great." My cousins' enchanted cakes always do. Not only are the base recipes delicious, but the positive emotions they imbibe into them also leave the consumer feeling great. While most of them are exclusive to the bakery, they let me sell a selection to go along with my coffee.

"And your baklava is here." She points to the smallest box at the top of her stack. "Has someone requested it? You don't normally want any."

"It's for a friend," I admit, glancing at the teapot.

Affection rolls off it, as if Azíl is paying attention to the conversation. He said he wasn't able to see when he was inside, but he hadn't said anything else about hearing. I wonder if he can?

"I didn't realise Sabine liked baklava," Clover says.

"I do have other friends," I counter.

She raises an eyebrow that screams disbelief. "Unless you're dating someone."

"I'm not."

"That's a shame, you haven't since that doctor."

"And if I remember correctly, none of you liked him," I remind her.

"Oh, we didn't. You can do way better."

I shake my head in amusement. "Good to know. Did you add all of these to the inventory already?" I gesture to the boxes.

"I did, you just have to sell them."

"Great, thanks, Clo."

"Anyway, I'd better be getting going, cakes don't sell themselves, you know."

"You could always use magic to make them do that."

"Rowen would never go for it, she's such a stickler for the rules," Clover laments as if her older sister is the only thing getting in the way of using magic to sell their cakes.

"There aren't any rules that go against, are there?"

"Only Rowen's, you know what she's like."

"Very true." There's a reason she's the one in charge of the bakery, and it's not an age thing.

"Anyway, see you later. Thanks for the tea." She waves and heads back towards the door.

"Who was that?" Aisha asks as she steps back behind the counter.

"My cousin, She makes the cakes."
I take the box of baklava off the top

and stick it to the side. If Aisha wasn't watching, I'd probably put it on the shelf next to Azíl's teapot, but it's better not to draw attention to him yet.

"Oh, do you not buy them in from a supplier?"

"My cousins run Broomstick Bakery down the street. Do you know it?" I pull on a disposable glove so I can transfer things easier.

"No."

I frown. That's unusual. The town centre isn't very big, and the bakery has gained a loyal following up and down the country, it seems strange that someone who lives here doesn't know it.

"You should try one of these, then you'll know it," I say. "What do you prefer, brownies or cupcakes?"

"Brownies. I love chocolate," she responds.

I flip open the box, releasing the delicious scent of rich chocolate into the air. "They make them with magic too, they're called pep-in-your-step brownies."

Aisha eyes the box warily. "What will they do to me?"

"Nothing much. They'll just make you feel bright. It's hard to explain if you've never had one, but they won't do anything bad."

"Okay." She dips her hand into the box and pulls one out, taking a deep bite. "Mmm, that's good. Is it the magic making it tasty?"

I shake my head. "That's the baking itself. The magic is just an extra."

"It's amazing."

"I have very talented cousins."

"Is that where you got the idea for the magic shots in the coffee?" she asks, gesturing to the syrups that line the shelves behind the coffee machine.

"More or less. It's something their grandmother used to do in her baking before she passed the bakery on to my cousins. She told us all about it before she passed and I started to wonder about it."

"She didn't think you should be part of the bakery too?"

I shake my head. "I'm not related to her. Our shared grandparents are both accountants, which isn't quite as interesting." Besides, I have my own inheritance from my Grandpa in the form of my coffee shop.

"You must be close if they're selling their cakes in your coffee shop," Aisha observes.

A small smile tugs at my face. "I'd like to think so."

Before we can continue the conversation, a customer approaches.

"I'll get it," Aisha says. "I need the practice."

"Be my guest." I have cakes to put in the display cases anyway.

I glance at Azíl, hoping he's okay trapped in his teapot. I suppose he can come out if he wants, but I don't think he will when so many people are around.

A sense of longing comes from the pot, and I realise that may be what he wants after all.

"I'm just going to take a break," I say to Aisha, grabbing both the teapot and the baklava from where I left it. "I'll be back."

She waves goodbye to me but doesn't say anything. It's just as well, I'm not sure how I'd be able to explain this one to her.

Chapter 8

I feel like a teenager sneaking around behind their parents' backs as I enter the storage room and set Azíl's teapot down on the table.

"It's safe to come out," I say. "No one else is here."

As if by magic, or more accurately, exactly like magic, he appears from the teapot in a puff of maroon smoke.

"If you don't want people to think that you're a genie, you may want to work on how you appear out of the teapot," I say dryly.

He chuckles and cricks his neck. "I have no control over that. And I would make a poor genie, I cannot do any magic."

"Because you don't have a wand?"

He shrugs. "I am not sure. I have not touched a wand since mine was...since the teapot became my home."

I frown. That almost makes it sound like his wand wasn't taken from him by choice. Which in turn implies that he wasn't trapped in the teapot by choice either.

I pull out my wand and hold it out to him. "Do you want to try?"

"You would let me touch your wand?"

I resist the urge to laugh, especially because he probably won't understand the joke. From the few conversations we've had already, I've discovered that while his English is excellent, his understanding of modern jokes and euphemisms is poor at best.

"I trust you not to place a curse on me," I say, realising the words are true even without having to think about them.

Gingerly, he reaches out and takes it from me, his fingers almost coming into contact with mine.

"What spell should I do?"

"Why don't you try an old favourite?" I suggest. "That way it's something you're comfortable with."

He nods and holds out my wand. Taking a deep breath he flicks it.

Nothing happens.

He repeats the action.

Nothing.

Disappointment flits over his face and he holds my wand back out to me. "Thank you for letting me try."

"I'm sorry it didn't work."

Azíl offers me a weak smile, but I can see in his eyes how it's making him feel. "I did not think it would. Before the teapot was my home, I could feel my magic here." He presses a fist against his chest. "Do you know what I mean?"

I nod. I can feel mine in the exact position he's referring to.

"Now, I cannot feel it. But it is nice to know for sure."

My heart aches for him. I can't imagine what it must be like to live without magic after having it. I glance down at my hands, only realising once I do that I'm still holding the box of baklava. And it's probably a good thing I am, it'll give us a good change of subject.

"I asked my cousin to bring some baklava around," I say. "I thought you might like it. She makes it with honey, nuts, and pastry, and you said you liked honey." I clear my throat feeling like I'm rambling.

I slide the box onto the table.

"You got this for me?" He seems both touched and surprised by the gesture, which only makes my heart hurt for him more. He must be lonely living in his teapot the way he is.

"If you don't like it, that's okay, but I thought you might want to try it."

"Thank you." He looks at the box before slowly opening the lid. "Do you want to have some with me?" He holds it out to me.

Four different types of baklava sit inside, though I don't know enough about it to know which is which. Clover must have just wanted to cover her bases with what she brought me.

"How about we share?" I offer before realising what I'm doing. "That way you can try all of them." If he has a favourite, then I can ask Clover to bring some more.

He smiles widely. "I'd like that."

I turn to the shelf with bamboo cutlery on it. I rarely need it, but I prefer to have takeaway options available in case someone asks, and this is more environmentally friendly than plastic.

I pick up one of the knives and grab a plate. I carefully cut each of the pieces of baklava in half, trying not to make too much of a mess, but my fingers still end up covered in honey despite that.

I step back and gesture for him to take his half. I don't go for my own straight away, choosing to watch him instead. I'm not sure if that makes me particularly weird, but I want to make sure he's actually enjoying it, and not just saying he is because I got him something.

He bites into the first piece and his eyes almost roll back in his head. "That is delicious."

I can't help the wide smile that spreads over my face. From what he's said, it sounds like he's had very little joy in the past three thousand years, it makes me happy to think that I can bring him some, even if it's only something as small as pieces of baklava.

"Which did you have?" I ask. "I want to make sure I eat the same one first."

He points to one with a slight green tint to it. If I have to guess, it's pistachio.

As I bite into it, I wonder if Clover gave me the kind with magic or without. I should have asked. Then again, even if it has magic, it may not work on Azíl, especially as he says he doesn't have to eat unless he wants to anyway.

The deliciously flakey pastry combined with the sweetness of the honey and the crunch of the nuts creates a beautiful mix in my mouth. Baklava isn't my favourite, but I can see how people would keep coming back to Clover again and again for more of this. It's divine.

We quickly finish the rest of it, talking about the different flavours.

"Thank you for getting this for me," he says earnestly. "I wish I could repay you."

"There's no need," I promise. "We swap baking and coffee all the time. It's one of the perks of having cousins who run a bakery."

"What else do they make there?" he asks.

"All kinds of things. Biscuits, tarts,

macarons, croissants, cupcakes. We have some more stuff in the display cases in the shop if you want to try some of it once we're alone again?"

"I should not eat your profit."

"You won't," I promise. "Unless you plan on eating and drinking everything in sight."

Azíl chuckles. "That is not my plan. I do not even know if I *can* eat that much."

"Considering it would make anyone who did it feel sick, I'm going to go with no."

"Then it seems like your coffee and cake are safe."

The smile I give him is a genuine one, and I feel like the one aimed in my direction is too. I like talking to the man from the teapot, even if we did meet in a bit of an unconventional way.

The echo of footsteps sounds from outside the storage room, and I freeze for a moment, wondering if it's someone going to the bathroom, or if it's Aisha coming to collect something. I probably shouldn't be in here much longer, it's unfair to leave her on her own for too long.

The moment the door handle starts to turn, I leap into action, reaching out and grabbing Azíl's jacket. I pull him behind the nearest shelf so Aisha doesn't see him when she comes in and starts asking questions I can't answer.

I can hear him breathing and feel his heart pounding with how close we are together, and it's only then that I realise I didn't think we could touch until this moment. I reacted on instinct instead of thinking things through.

Our gazes meet, and something changes in the air around us, though I can't put my finger on what it is.

I glance down to find my fingers still curled in the fabric of his jacket.

"Sorry," I whisper ever so softly, letting go of it.

He smiles gently at me, and I know he's telling me that it's okay without saying anything out loud.

"Willow, are you in here?" Aisha calls. "I'm looking for some more cream, but I can't find it."

I curse. This means I'm going to have to explain what I'm doing hiding behind a shelf.

I gesture for Azíl to step back a little and notice the small chalkboard signs sitting on a shelf behind him. I grab one of them and step out into the storage room. "Hey, I was just grabbing one of these for the brownies." I hold it up so she can see. "The cream's in the walk-in fridge next door." I put a smile on my face, hoping it covers the nervousness I'm feeling.

"Oh, right. I should have known. Thanks." Her gaze slips to the teapot and the empty box next to it, but she doesn't question it.

Either she knows something, or she thinks I'm really weird. The latter would be better, I don't want her questioning Azíl's teapot any more than she has to.

The door closes behind her and I breathe a sigh of relief.

Azíl steps out from behind the shelves. "That was close. I should have gone back into my teapot."

"Why didn't you?" I honestly hadn't considered that as an option until he said it.

"I thought that might be too noticeable."

I nod. He's probably right. "Why don't you do that now and I'll hide the teapot until the coffee shop is locked up tonight?" I suggest. "I don't know why, but I don't want to take it back out front right now."

To my surprise, he nods. "I understand why you feel that way. Something doesn't seem right."

"No, it doesn't." But I can't tell exactly why. Hopefully, I won't have to wait too long to find out.

Chapter 9

I collapse onto the sofa and groan, covering my eyes with my hands.

"Was your day that bad?" Azíl asks.

"Oh, I hadn't noticed you come out of your pot."

He chuckles. "Then I am getting better at doing it without noticing. I hope you are not bothered by it, I do not want to make you uncomfortable in your own home."

"That's sweet, but I promise it's fine." But now he mentions it, I realise how strange that is. He's basically a stranger to me, but I'm comfortable with him staying in my space, eating my food, and seeing every aspect of my life.

Even thinking about it doesn't make me want to run for the hills.

"There's something I'm curious about," I say.

"What is it? If I can answer, then I will."

"What happened that trapped you in the teapot?"

Silence follows my question. Maybe I shouldn't have asked, but it's been bugging me ever since I met Azíl and I feel like knowing the answer could make a difference to *something*. Though I'm yet to work out what that thing is.

He lets out a long sigh. "You want to know?"

I nod and sit up straight. "But if it's uncomfortable for you to tell me, that's okay, I understand."

"No, it is not that." He pushes a hand through his hair, though I'd never be able to tell it's what he's done as the dark curls spring back into place easily. "It is not a very nice story."

"So you were trapped by someone else. I figured that would probably have been the case."

Surprise flits across his face. "What makes you think that?"

"A couple of things you've said, but mostly the fact you can't do magic. I find it unlikely that any warlock would willingly be confined to such a small space without their wand."

He nods. "You would be right."

"So what happened?"

"I was the chief warlock in our clan, this was the days before magic became hidden, it is nice to see that the acceptance of supernaturals has come to pass again."

I nod. "I don't like the idea of having to hide such a big part of who I am," I agree.

"Our clan chief was a fair but ruthless man. He did not like the idea of anyone going against him. Most of the time, it was not an issue, but then he decided to marry off his daughter."

"Were you in love with her?" I ask

as something akin to jealousy mounts inside me. I don't like the way it makes me feel, so I push it down.

"Oh, no. We grew up together and were friends, but nothing more. Nor did either of us want to be."

I don't know why, but I'm relieved at the revelation.

"He made a deal with another clan chief that she would marry his son, and she was set against it, wanting nothing to do with the deal or either of the men," Azíl continues.

"The poor woman."

A sad smile crosses his face. "A few days before the wedding, she came to ask me for a favour in the dead of night. She wanted me to create a mark on her face, so that the wedding would not go ahead." He touches his cheek as he recalls the memory.

"And you did it."

"I did. She was distraught and I knew that no amount of reasoning would convince her father to stop the wedding. She promised she would not reveal that it was me who had cast the spell, but I knew there would be no question about it. Her father would know it was me regardless of what either of us said."

"Did the wedding go ahead?"

He shakes his head. "The other clan chief took one look at her face and swore revenge against whoever did it."

"Was he the one who trapped you in the teapot?" I glance in the direction of the object in question, trying to imagine what it must be like to be stuck there for so long.

"No. It was my own clan chief and the junior warlocks who had previously been under my command. They came in the middle of the night and made sure my wand was not in reach. Even so, it took five of them to bind me in the teapot, and their descendants have spent their lives trying to keep me confined ever since."

"The curse didn't completely work?" I ask.

He sighs. "I imagine the curse was never designed to last this long at all. Every few hundred years, the enchantment wears off enough that I can come out if someone uses magic on the teapot."

"Like what I did."

"Exactly, though it has been less than a hundred years since I was last free. Perhaps the last person to cast the curse did not do a very good job."

"I imagine there has to be a lot of bad intent to cast a good curse," I respond. "If they didn't understand why they were doing it, then they might not have done a good job."

"Perhaps. I am not sure."

"So every few hundred years you've appeared to someone?"

"More or less. It means that I have been able to keep up with the world. Sometimes, people have kept the teapot on shelves while it has been sealed, which has let me do the same thing," he says.

"But the descendants of the people

who cursed you always find you and put you back in the teapot?"

He nods.

"That's awful. They don't have anything against you, they shouldn't be upholding a punishment like this." I hate the idea that someone is going to come along and force him back into his teapot.

And not just because then I won't get to see him again.

"I am being punished for what I did wrong."

"And do you feel guilty for it?" I sit up straighter, interested in hearing his answer, though I'm not sure what it will tell me about him.

He pauses, as if considering what to say. "No. I do not feel guilty. I know I should for crossing my chief, but I could not stand by and watch my friend suffer like that." Pain crosses his features as he says it, as if he feels guilty about not feeling guilty.

I get to my feet and make my way over to the other sofa, reaching out and putting my hand over his once I have.

"I think you did the right thing," I whisper. "And the right thing is sometimes hard."

He nods, but doesn't say anything.

"Do you know what happened to your friend?"

"No. I imagine she was punished, or one of the others removed the mark and she was punished by being forced into the marriage she did not want. But I have no idea what happened to her."

My heart constricts along with the pain in his voice. It's clear he hasn't forgiven himself for everything that happened.

"How can we free you from the curse?" I ask.

He looks up sharply, meeting my gaze. "Free me?"

I nod. "If you say the curse keeps wearing off, then there must be something that can be done to end it."

"It is hard without the counter-curse," he admits. "No one has ever succeeded in finding one before."

"I'm sorry they didn't."

"You do not need to be sorry. You have done nothing wrong."

"Neither have you, but you're being punished as if you have," I point out. "So, breaking the curse, do you have any ideas?"

He sighs. "No. I do not recall the curse they originally used. The only people who will know are the ones who recast it, and even they may not have the original."

"Well, that just makes it more difficult then. But I promise we'll find a way to end this so you can live as a free warlock again."

"That may not be an option if one of the descendants returns for me."

Right. That is something I haven't taken into account. "Do you know who they are?"

"No. They never reveal any information about themselves."

"And even if they did, it would be a

name from the nineteen-twenties and not be much help to us now," I finish for him.

"Precisely."

"Okay. Then let's start with the obvious."

"Which is?" he prompts.

"We're going to ask Sabine if there are any hints about all of this where she found your teapot."

"Ah. The other woman who lives here?"

I nod. "You don't have to meet her if you don't want, I can talk to her on my own." I'm not sure how he's going to feel about interacting with other people.

"I will think about it."

I nod, completely understanding that this is hard for him, and that he needs time to adjust to the situation.

"I'd better get some dinner started. Do you want to eat?" I get to my feet.

"You will make some for me too?" He sounds surprised, as if I haven't been including him everywhere I can.

"If you want something, yes. If you don't, then no."

"I would."

"Okay, dinner is coming right up." I head to the kitchen, pleased I can do something that makes both of us feel normal.

Figuring out how to break a curse isn't something I've done before, but I think I can work it out.

No, I have to work it out. I won't stop until he's free of it, even if I'm not sure why I care so much.

I glance back into the living room and see Azíl sitting with a sad expression on his face.

Okay, so maybe I do know why I care so much. I like him, more than I should considering the weird way he came into my life. But it really is as simple as that.

Chapter 10

The fresh scent of mint leaves fills the air as I place a teapot full of Moroccan mint tisane in the centre of the table. Azíl let slip that this is the drink he often had important conversations while drinking before he was cursed, and I want him to feel as comfortable as possible when talking to Sabine. Especially because I don't know how she's going to respond.

Then again, I shouldn't worry about that too much. Sabine sees weird things all the time because of her job, she's not going to think a cursed warlock is particularly strange.

The coffee shop door opens and my friend walks in with a big goofy smile on her face.

"Good day with Sawyer?" I ask despite promising myself that I wouldn't tease her too much about the fact she seems to be falling back in love with her academy ex.

She lets out a happy sigh. "Yep."

"Wow, you're not even going to deny it."

"You wouldn't believe me even if I did," she points out.

"True." I flick my wand towards the door and turn the sign so it says opening again soon.

"What did you want me to come in for? Shouldn't there be people in at this time?"

I shake my head. "It's always dead around now, and there's something I need to talk to you about. I was going to do it when you came home last night, but I fell asleep before you did." I gesture for her to take a seat.

"There are three tea glasses."

"Yes. So, the teapot." I reach out and put my hand on the ornate one containing Azíl and not the glass one with our brewing tea. Warmth radiates off it from my touch, and I have to assume it's coming from the man inside.

"This is about the teapot again?" She raises an eyebrow and leans back in her chair. "Is it getting jealous again?"

I give a low chuckle. "I don't think so. But I do have an explanation for why that happened."

"Now I'm intrigued."

"I don't really know where to start," I admit. "It might be easier to just show you." I tap twice on the side of the teapot, the signal I agreed with Azíl before he went back inside.

A puff of maroon smoke immediately fills the air, causing Sabine to cough and splutter.

Oops. I should have warned her.

Azíl pops into being beside me and gives my best friend an odd little bow.

Sabine squeaks.

"This is Azíl," I say, gesturing to him. "He lives in the teapot." Now there's a sentence I never thought I'd say.

"Lives. Teapot." She points between the two, then realises what she's doing and clears her throat. "I'm sorry, you took me by surprise and I'm being rude. Hello, Azíl, it's nice to meet you." She's flustered, but I can tell that she's putting the pieces together.

"It is a pleasure to meet you too," he says, taking the free seat.

I pour us each a glass of the mint tisane, and hand their glasses to them.

Azíl's fingers brush against mine as he takes his, and my mouth goes a little dry.

I pull away, trying not to think about it.

"Anyway, Azíl has been living in the teapot you found on your dig," I say.

Her eyes widen. "But I didn't feel a spirit inside that."

"You would not be able to feel my spirit anyway," Azíl responds. "I am a warlock."

Sabine shifts uncomfortably. "I'd be able to sense a warlock ghost."

Awe and adoration cross Azíl's face. "You are a necromancer," he says with certainty. "I never thought I would get the privilege of meeting one. You must forgive me for my rude appearance." He bows in his chair.

Sabine exchanges a perplexed glance with me. Somewhere along the lines, necromancers have stopped being seen that way. But that's a conversation to have with Azíl at another time.

"We were wondering if there was anything at the dig site that might help us get to the bottom of Azíl's curse."

She shakes her head almost immediately. "I don't think so. The thing about Azíl's teapot is that it was so different from the rest of the treasures found at the dig site. We actually had questions about how it got there in the first place."

"I can answer that question," Azíl responds. "I am not sure if that will help."

"I'm an archaeologist, wanting answers is my job," Sabine counters, already warming up to him.

"My teapot was put there after the last time my curse was renewed. The descendants of the original curse casters did not want the responsibility of guarding the teapot, so they decided to seal me in a place they thought no one would disturb."

"When was that?" she asks.

"Some time in the nineteen-twenties," he says.

A small snort escapes Sabine. "They put you in an Egyptian temple at the height of the Egyptology craze so that you wouldn't be easily found?"

"It worked for a hundred years," I point out. I take a sip of my tea. It's not my normal drink of choice, but it goes down easily, and feels like the perfect accompaniment to the conversation.

"True, but that feels more like luck

than planning," she says. "You can visit the things we recovered at the museum in Birmingham next month, if that helps? They're doing a tour of the country before being sent back to Egypt."

I perk up. "We can see them ourselves?"

She nods. "I can probably get you tickets for the opening event if you want?"

"Please?"

"I'll see what I can do. You'll need two, right?"

"That would be best." I suppose Azíl could just enter in his teapot and come out then, but it might be nice for him to walk into an event as a proper guest.

"I seem to have been lucky that this is where you sent me, and that Willow has been so kind," Azíl says to Sabine. "I must thank you."

Her eyes widen. "You're the one who asked me to send you here."

"I asked you to take me somewhere

safe," he corrects. "This is where you thought of."

Sabine glances at me and blushes.

I reach out and give her hand a squeeze, letting her know that I don't mind that she thought of our home as safe.

"This is home," Sabine says. "I know I don't spend much time here, but this is always where I think of."

A smile spreads over my face. "I'm glad, I want you to feel at home. This is where you legally live."

She chuckles. "That's true. Though it seems I've picked up a second room-mate by accident."

"I do not take up much space," Azíl jokes, gesturing to his teapot.

It takes us both off guard for a moment, but then we laugh, and I notice how easy it feels. Azíl has a way about him that makes people feel comfortable. It doesn't surprise me that his chief's daughter turned to him to help her. I would do too.

I turn in his direction and watch

him for a moment, enjoying the way the sun lights up his dark skin. Intelligence and thoughtfulness sparkle in his eyes. Three thousand years of being trapped in a teapot could have made him twisted and bitter, but instead, he seems to have weathered it as someone who wouldn't hurt a fly.

The fact that people have been trapping him like this for so long fills me with an anger unlike any I've ever felt before.

"I'm sorry I can't help more," Sabine says. "But I have access to some books that the general public can't, I can look up some of the curses and spells from around the era Azíl was cursed and see if I can find something that might be helpful. You need the exact curse to be able to undo it, right?"

I sigh. "Yes. There are rumours that someone has figured out how to create countercurses without it, but I don't think we can afford their fee."

Sabine's eyes widen. "You might

not need to pay a fee," she says. "Leave it with me, and I'll see what you can do."

"Okay..." Why is she being so cryptic? I trust her, but it does raise more questions.

Before I can prompt her to expand further, the door creaks open and the bell rings.

"I'm sorry, we're closed until, oh, Aisha, hi." How am I going to explain what's going on here?

A soft pop sounds beside me, and I don't have to look to know that Azíl has disappeared back into his teapot. I don't think he realises that it looks more suspicious for him to disappear from sight than it does to just sit there.

"Are you expecting someone else?" Aisha asks as she reaches us.

"Oh, no, this is just my friend Sabine, she lives upstairs. Sabine, this is Aisha, my new barista."

"It's nice to finally meet you," Sabine says.

"Likewise," Aisha responds. "I was

only asking because there are three glasses."

"Oh, right. I must have poured another one by accident," I lie. And not very well. Why couldn't he have just stayed visible? I realise he doesn't want people to know he lives in a teapot, but I don't think anyone would assume that unless they actually saw him coming in and out of it.

"Ah. I'm just going to go put my stuff in the back and then I'll start setting up for the next lot of customers. Are we staying closed for long?" Aisha asks.

I sigh. "No, we're opening back up now." I flick my wand in the direction of the door, flipping the sign back to open. We won't be finishing our conversation now she's here, and there's no point missing out on trade. "Well, I guess it's time for me to get back to work."

Sabine nods. "I'll do what I promised." She glances at the teapot. "Can he hear us?"

I nod.

She clears her throat and glances to make sure Aisha isn't within earshot. "Goodbye, Azíl. I look forward to seeing you again."

Something like a farewell floats off the teapot.

"He says goodbye," I translate.

She raises an eyebrow.

"Don't look at me like that, you're the one who sent me a man trapped in a teapot."

"I didn't do it on purpose," she reminds me.

"But it is still your fault."

"All right, I'll take entire responsibility for the handsome and charming man currently living in your teapot."

A blush rises to my cheeks, but I ignore it and pretend it isn't happening. "Technically, it's his teapot."

Sabine lets out a light laugh. "I'll see you later. Don't do anything I wouldn't do."

"That doesn't leave me with very much off the table," I quip.

"No, it doesn't." She all but winks at me.

I shake my head in amusement and shoo her out of the coffee shop, leaving me to the rest of my day.

Chapter 11

Customers come and go, and the coffee machine whirs as it gets used countless times in a row.

Every now and again, I glance at Azíl's pot, wishing he could be out of it and enjoy the sights and sounds that life has to offer. I know why he isn't going to, but that doesn't change the fact that I want things to be different for him.

And I will make them different.

It's non-stop until we finally hit a lull where there are only a couple of customers in the corner of the coffee shop, and neither of them are paying us much attention.

"I'm just grabbing some milk," I tell Aisha as I head back to the fridge. Now that it's a bit quieter, we need to set up for the next rush, and milk is always one of the first things to go.

I stare into the fridge for a moment, realising that I'm not enjoying work quite as much as I normally do now I have something more interesting to do when I go home at the end of the day. Talking to Azíl has become the highlight of my day, whether I'm trying to teach him something about the way the new world works, or if he's telling me about one of the many people who he's befriended over the years. Some of his stories are sad, others could be made into movies, they're so enter-taining.

I wonder which I'll be if I don't manage to figure out a counter curse for him?

I push the thought aside. I'm not going to entertain the notion that I won't manage. I don't plan on stopping until he's free.

The moment I step back behind the counter, I freeze, noticing that Aisha is almost touching the teapot and I can feel the discomfort coming from Azíl in waves. I guess that answers whether he just likes everyone who picks up the pot.

I clear my throat.

Aisha jumps back, looking guilty only for a split second before dusting herself off and plastering on a fake smile. "Oh, you're there. I was just wondering what to do with these glasses, they don't look like the other ones." She holds one out to me.

I frown, not recognising them. I set the milk down and reach out for the glass. She lets go just as I'm about to take it, and the glass falls to the ground, smashing into thousands of tiny pieces.

My eyes close without me thinking about it, protecting them from any fragments hitting and hurting me.

The ring of the bell goes as our only customers leave.

"I can get it," Aisha says, withdrawing her wand just after I've pulled out my own.

"It's fine." I circle my wand above the glass, collecting the pieces and making them head towards the recycling bin. "I guess that saves us from having to work out where it came from."

She gives a short, sharp laugh. "True."

One of the pieces of glass slips and falls out of the line of shards, which is unusual but not unheard of. Once the rest are safely in the bin, I lean down to pick it up. To my surprise, I find myself fumbling with it, and a small rivulet of blood drips down my finger.

Huh. That's odd. I don't normally manage to cut myself.

Before I can wipe it away, a strange sense of peace settles over me, almost like the world is fuzzy around me. I don't normally react to blood this way, but it could be a strange reaction.

"You will listen to me," Aisha says, her voice faint and dreamlike. "Tell me everything."

I frown. "Everything?"

"Where did you get this teapot from?" She gestures to it as if I need any help telling which teapot she's asking about.

"It was a gift." Didn't I tell her this before? Why is she asking about this now?

"Don't lie."

I frown. "Why would I lie?" I get to my feet, having to reach out and steady myself against the counter so I don't fall over.

Why do I feel so weird?

"You must be lying."

"I'm not lying. My friend sent it to me."

"Your friend Sabine?" Aisha asks.

"Yes, Sabine."

The teapot shakes as if Azíl is trying to warn me of something. But what? I don't know what's happening well enough to stop anything.

"Where is she from?" Aisha asks, pulling my attention back to her.

My gaze fixates on a small circular pin with a line through it on her lapel, but I can't work out what it's of. "Here," I respond. "She lives here."

Aisha groans in frustration. "I know she lives here. Where is she from originally?"

"Here," I repeat. "We went to the academy together."

Something tells me that I'm not giving her the answers she wants. I don't understand why I'm answering her at all at this point.

"Where did she get the teapot from?"

"I'm not sure." I don't know exactly why I know I need to tell the partial truth and not the whole truth, but I'm certain of it in this moment.

The emotions coming off Azíl's teapot are making me more and more concerned. He doesn't seem to like something that's happening, and I'm not sure what. But focusing on how he's feeling makes my head a little bit clearer.

"Who are you?" I ask.

"What?"

"Who are you?" I repeat. "Why are you asking all of these questions of me?"

"I..." She trails off, probably because she doesn't want to answer. Which is a shame, because I want to know.

Things come back into focus more now that she's been caught off guard, making me feel as if I'm more in control. I step forward and reach out a hand for Azíl's teapot, certain that his emotions are one of the things that are keeping me grounded right now.

The moment I touch it, all of the fog clears away and I'm able to think clearly again. I let out a sigh of relief but press my hand to my head to cover it. I don't want her to think I've thrown off whatever she's using on me.

"You know, I'm feeling a bit light-headed, blood does that to me," I lie. She doesn't know it's not true, so I feel like I can get away with it. "Why don't you head home and I'll close up. Don't worry, you'll get a full day's pay still."

She stares at me, probably a little confused about what's going on.

"All right, I'll grab my stuff." She gives me a forced smile and heads to the staffroom.

A queasy feeling fills me, but I push past it, knowing I need to stay focused until she's out of the coffee shop and I'm on my own.

My whole body tenses as Aisha reappears, but she hurries to the door without saying a word to me.

I wait until she's out of sight and flick my wand in that direction, locking the doors and pulling down the blinds. It's a shame I'll have to miss out on the trade, but I need to work out what just happened.

And clear my head. I'm really not feeling too good.

"You can come out now," I say to Azíl. "Everyone is..." Before I can finish my sentence, my vision fades and the last thing I'm aware of is a cloud of maroon smoke and the feeling of safety that accompanies it.

Chapter 12

I rub my eyes and sit up, still feeling a little groggy but managing to think at least a little.

"You are awake," Azíl says. "Here." He passes me a mug of what looks like tea.

"Thanks." I take it from him and sit back, realising I'm on the sofa upstairs instead of down in the coffee shop. "Did you bring me up here?"

He nods. "I hope that is all right. I thought you would be more comfortable. I checked the door was locked before I came up though." He hovers as if he wants to sit next to me, but doesn't want to impose.

I reach out and tug on his sleeve.

The teapot sits on the coffee table, close enough that it's not going to impede him moving around, but not attached to him. I wonder how far he can go from it, I've never actually asked, but I can't imagine it's far.

"Thank you, Azíl," I say softly once he's seated. "I really appreciate it, I don't know what happened."

"She used blood magic on you."

My eyebrows knit together. "Blood magic? I didn't think she was a necromancer." She doesn't feel the same way Sabine does to me.

"No, it is still witch and warlock magic, but it is ancient and frowned upon. She was using your blood to compel you to obey her."

My eyes widen. "What? Why?"

"I do not know."

"She was asking about your pot. She didn't do anything to you while I was out of the room, did she?"

I set my mug of tea down and turn to him, worry pouring out of every part of me as I search his face for any signs that something bad has happened.

His gaze softens as he looks back at me, and he reaches out to push away a strand of my dark hair.

"I am fine," he promises. "Are you?"

I nod. "Just worried." And not doing anything to move away from his touch. I like it more than I thought I would.

No. That's inaccurate. I like it more than I would if anyone else was the one doing it.

"I was scared," he admits.

"I'm sorry, maybe I shouldn't have taken you down to the coffee shop, I just thought it would be better if you could enjoy the world, even if it is from a shelf."

To my surprise, he chuckles. "I was not scared because of what she might do to me."

"Oh. Then what scared you?"

"The idea that she might hurt you."

My breathing hitches and my gaze meets his. There's something very earnest hiding there, he means what he's saying, every word of it.

I bite my bottom lip and his gaze flicks down to it, revealing more than I think he wants to about the situation.

He clears his throat and starts to turn away.

"Azíl." I reach out and touch his chest, forcing his attention back to me. "What were you just thinking about?"

"Something very improper," he admits.

"By your standards, or by mine?"

"I think that depends on your thoughts about the matter," he responds carefully, searching me for any sign that he might be going down the wrong path.

"If you don't tell me what you're thinking, then I can't tell you that," I point out.

He chuckles. "You are very intelligent."

"I wouldn't say very, but thank you."

"I was thinking about how it would feel to kiss you," he admits.

My heart flutters at the idea. "I think that's only improper by your standards," I say quietly. "It's quite all right by mine."

He arches an eyebrow. "If you are sure?"

"Azíl, if you want to kiss me, then you can kiss me," I say firmly, barely thinking about anything other than that.

"I should warn you that it has been a very long time since I kissed anyone," he says. "I may have forgotten how."

I resist the urge to roll my eyes. "I don't imagine you can be that bad of a kisser."

Despite his words, he shifts closer on the sofa. A sensation of shyness washes over me, but it isn't unpleasant. It's the feeling I get when something big is going to happen in my life and there's no way to stop it.

Not that I want to.

I want this.

Azíl freezes, and I realise that if we both want this, then I'm going to have to be the one who initiates it properly.

I reach up and cup his cheek in my hand. His short beard tickles my palm, but in a pleasant way that makes me wonder what it'll be like when we kiss.

The air around us changes and it's full of the promise of things to come. I lean in, my eyes fluttering closed as he slips an arm around my waist, pulling me closer. It's the most we've touched, and it's worth it. Every nerve in my body feels like it's tingling from the anticipation.

The moment his lips meet mine, a sense of connection and rightness settle into place within me. There's no other way for me to describe it. There is just something about it that feels right.

We break apart and stare at one another, neither of us saying a word.

I reach up and touch my lips, realising they're still tingling. "You certainly haven't forgotten how to kiss," I murmur.

He flashes me a boyish smile, seeming almost lighter than he has the rest of the time I've known him. "So now in the traditions of my people, we are married," he announces.

My eyes widen and I splutter. "What?"

He bursts out laughing, and I realise he's pulling my leg.

"This time, I am sorry," he says. "That was a mean joke."

"It was a little." I let out a small laugh, seeing the funny side. "I don't think it would be possible to marry someone cursed in either of our cultures."

"Hmm, you may be correct. I suppose that gives us plenty of time to get to know one another better."

I narrow my eyes at him. "You realise you're going to ruin modern men for me, right?"

"Perhaps I want to do that," he teases. "Or I hope that you would already have high standards that they cannot meet."

"Ah, so it is your plan to ruin them."

"You would be worth it."

"I'm the only person you've met recently, maybe you're just feeling this way because of that."

"I do not think so. But if that is your fear, then I can meet some more people so you can be sure I mean what I say," he announces.

"You'd do that for me?"

"I will do it for me," he counters. "You want to free me from my curse, which means I will have to learn to live in this time. Perhaps I should start now so that I can learn how to go about that. You will probably need a new barista, right?"

"You want to work for me?"

"If you don't mind?"

"Are you sure?" Excitement thrums through me at the idea of being able to actually talk to him throughout the day. "You've wanted to stay in your teapot so I thought you'd want to continue doing so."

"A part of me does wish to," he responds. "But I also know that I cannot hide forever, and that it is unfair of me to put you in danger because I cannot defend myself. I want to be with you next time something like this happens."

I reach out and take his hand in mine, giving him a reassuring smile. "If you're sure, then I'm all for it. But all you have to say is one word and you can go back in your teapot."

"Thank you," he says. "But I'm ready to face the world. You've helped me do that, Willow, and I'm grateful for it."

A sense of contentment settles within me at his words. "I look forward to it."

Thank you for reading *Pumpkin Spice And All Things Nice*, I hope you enjoyed it! Willow and Azíl's story will continue in *Hazelnut Latte And Something To Say:* http://books2read.com/hazelnutlatte andsomethingtosay

You can also read Azíl's point of view of the events of chapter 5 here: https://books.authorlauragreenwood. co.uk/d877oy0t7u

Author Note

Thank you for reading *Pumpkin Spice And All Things Nice*, I hope you enjoyed the first part of Willow and Azíl's story. This one has been a long time in the making coming to you, and I'm really excited to have it out in the world so the characters can have their say.

If you're interested in the *Broomstick Bakery* and Willow's cousins, then they have their own series (of the same name) in which they all find romance. And if you want to know more about how curses in *The Obscure World* work, then you can in *Grimalkin Academy*, which follows 18-year-old Mona as she struggles with a curse that means she produces kittens every time she does a spell (Mona will also be making an appearance later in the *Cauldron Coffee Shop* series!)

Two of the characters in the book are actually named after real people - Sabine is a friend who once complained that there were no non-evil characters named Sabine, and so I promised to write one for her (by the way, you can find Sabine and Sawyer's story in *Unfortunate Decrees and Iced Coffees*!) The other is Spooky, who is based on a cat who my partner and I actually did nickname Spooky after the way she's come and go into our house without warning. She's not our cat, but she certainly acted like she was!

If you want to keep up to date with new releases and other news, you can join my Facebook Reader Group or mailing list.

Stay safe & happy reading!
- Laura

The excavation may be plagued by the bad luck brought about by the stone, but at least things aren't quite so bad for Sabine's love life…

-

Unfortunate Decrees and Iced Coffees is a companion story of the Cauldron Coffee Shop urban fantasy series. It includes a stubborn necromancer archeologist, a mysterious stone, a handsome warlock, and a second chance romantic subplot.

If you love cozy urban fantasy, coffee shop settings, low-stakes adventures, cat familiars, and a warm and fuzzy feeling vibe, start the Cauldron Coffee Shops series with Pumpkin Spice And All Things Nice.

You can get your free copy of Unfortunate Decrees and Iced Coffees here: https://books.authorlauragreenwood.co.uk/sabine

Also by Laura Greenwood

You can find out more about each of my series on my website.

- The Apprentice Of Anubis: an urban fantasy series set in an alternative world where the Ancient Egyptian Empire never fell. It follows a new apprentice to the temple of Anubis as she learns about her new role.
- Forgotten Gods: a paranormal adventure romance series inspired by Egyptian mythology. Each book follows a different Ancient Egyptian goddess.
- Jinx Paranormal Dating Agency: a paranormal romance series based on worldwide mythology where paranormals and deities take part in events organised by the

Jinx Dating Agency. Each book follows a different couple.

- House Of Blood And Roses: a vampire romantasy series following a heroine who discovers she's a vampire noble and has to navigate a world full of politics, betrayal, and blood lust.
- Amethyst's Wand Shop Mysteries (with Arizona Tape): an urban fantasy murder mystery series following a witch who teams up with a detective to solve murders. Each book includes a different murder.
- Scales Of Justice: an urban fantasy following a thief who accidentally becomes the newest apprentice of the goddess of truth.
- Purple Oak Oasis (with Ariana Jade): a cozy fantasy romance series with unusual magic. Each book follows a different couple.
- Falhaven Castle: a cozy fantasy romance series following a princess who just wants to

bake, a slow burn friends-to-lovers romance, and an adorable baking dragon.

- Speed Dating With The Denizens Of The Underworld (shared world): a paranormal romance shared world based on mythology from around the world. Each book follows a different couple.

- Blackthorn Academy For Supernaturals (shared world): a paranormal monster romance shared world based at Blackthorn Academy. Each book follows a different couple.

You can find a complete list of all my books on my website:

https://books.authorlauragreenwood.co.uk/book-list

Signed Paperback & Merchandise:

You can find signed paperbacks, hardcovers, and merchandise based on my series (including stickers, magnets, face masks, and more!) via my website:

https://books.authorlauragreenwood.co.uk/shop

About Laura Greenwood

Laura is a USA Today Bestselling Author of paranormal romance, urban fantasy, and fantasy romance. When she's not writing, she drinks a lot of tea, tries to resist French macarons, and works towards a diploma in Egyptology. She lives in the UK, where most of her books are set. Laura specialises in quick reads, with healthy relationships and consent-positive moments regardless of if she's writing light-hearted romance, mythology-heavy urban fantasy, or anything in between.

Follow Laura Greenwood

- Website: www.authorlaura-greenwood.co.uk
- Mailing List: https://books.

authorlauragreenwood.co.uk/newsletter

- Facebook Group: http://facebook.com/groups/theparanormalcouncil
- Discord Server: https://discord.gg/W6zExZkUG6
- Facebook Page: http://facebook.com/authorlauragreenwood
- Bookbub: https://www.bookbub.com/authors/laura-greenwood